AuthorHouse™
1663 Liberty Drive
Bloomington, IN 47403
www.authorhouse.com
Phone: 1 (800) 839-8640

Published by AuthorHouse 05/08/2015

ISBN: 978-1-4969-6792-3 (sc)
ISBN: 978-1-4969-6791-6 (e)

Library of Congress Control Number: 2015901877

Print information available on the last page.

Any people depicted in stock imagery provided by Thinkstock are models,
and such images are being used for illustrative purposes only.
Certain stock imagery © Thinkstock.

This book is printed on acid-free paper.

More Cartoons:
Men & Women & Children
by Bernard Schoenbaum
Compiled by Rhoda A. Schoenbaum & LauraSchoenbaum

authorHOUSE®

Photo of Bernard at exhibition of his cartoons September 1994

Foreword

You may wonder why the title includes the word "More"?
Bernard Schoenbaum's cartoons have been published worldwide but upon
his death, hundreds of unpublished cartoons were found in his files.

To distinguish them from the already published cartoons, my daughter
Laura, a graphic designer, and I have organized them and compiled
some of them into the group included in this publication with the title of
More Cartoons : Men & Woman & Children

So here you have **More...**
Hope they bring smiles!

Rhoda A. Schoenbaum
2015

Men & Women

" *Money's my medium.* "

"It sure looks like you're getting that old confidence back!"

" *We were just wondering if you'd mind terribly if we borrowed your trained eye for just a moment ?* "

" *We tried everything but we fear it lost its will to go on.* "

"I never thought it would happen
but I've fallen in love with the little car again."

"Al, I've been coming here one year to the day. That calls for a celebration."

" To bartenders yet unborn."

" You'll like him. He places personal gain above happiness."

"I have it from a reliable sourse that this will be a major address."

"*Everything's on the table but still no breakthroughs.*"

"*Perk up dear, I'm sure you'll find someone to merge with.*"

" Still searching for loopholes, and you? "

"*I couldn't stand the heat in the kitchen.*"

" *Gentlemen, the story in a nutshell.* "

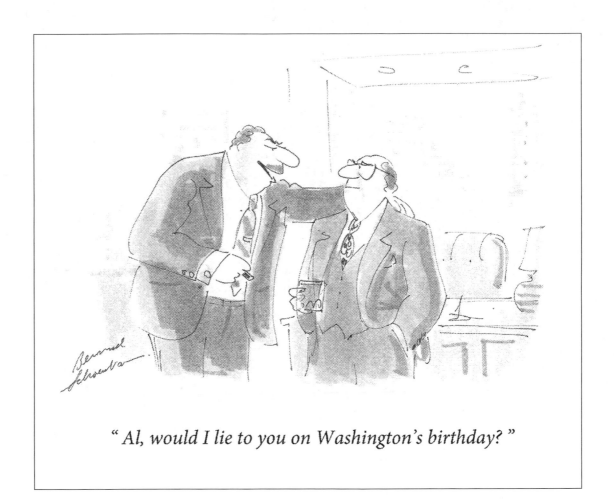

"Al, would I lie to you on Washington's birthday?"

"If I had to do it over again, I'd do it the same way."

" *Are you expecting a Mr. Kringle?* "

"The hardware maybe going
but the old software's as good as ever."

"It's my unpleasant duty to inform you that there is nothing to distribute in this will. The deceased has taken it with him."

"Yes, the attorney for the defense may bring forth his surprise witness."

" Have a lovely day in court dear and do try not to be too judgemental."

"*Your honor, I would like to introduce to the court as evidence the defendants very own words carved in stone.*"

" Hon, I'm downloading this evening in my memory forever."

" To streamline our service, we serve the check first."

"*Are you for or against the death penalty?*"

"Make it number 3, the 'up and at 'em' breakfast."

"*Alfredo, my palate's in your hands.*"

"Can you rush our order through?
We're from that generation of instant gratification."

" What shall it be, ' The Devil May Care' or
' Be Kind To Your Arteries ' menu? "

"*A few areas still remain unresolved, a breakthrough is imminent and payment should be forthcoming.*"

" *I'll have the stale bread and tap water.*"

" *Those are my suggestions*
but you're certainly entitled to a second opinion."

" *May I recommend Brahms with your cocktail Mozart for your entree and finally a little Vavaldi for desert ?*"

"*They call it a surprise; believe me it's no surprise.*"

" *This menu asks much too much of me.* "

"*That's my daughter and her husband, they would have been happily married ten years if they weren't divorced.*"

"Maybell, what I am asking is your hand in divorce."

"*I'd be careful. He suffers from delusions of adequacy.*"

"*I believe the young lady in the rear had her hand up first.*"

"*What say gentlmen, we put aside our charm and get down to substance.*"

" *Maxwell, how would you like to take some so called fresh thinking and give it that old twist of yours?* "

"*Let's throw them a curve and take the highroad today.*"

"We hope you like it. It's a page right from your book."

" *Ms. Williams, send in the fall guy.*"

" *Still waiting for things to turn around and you ?* "

"Hello...Anything out there that smacks of money?"

"*Let me get back to you. We're still checking the fundamentals.*"

"It's another 500 foot climb for a second opinion."

" Hold it. I've an update."

" *I'm looking for long term growth at minimum risk.* "

"*Are we ready, everyone? Say 'photosynthesis'.*"

"*How well do you hold up to scrutiny?*"

"There you go, hiding behind its constitutionality again."

" *Loved the way you clouded the issue.* "

"*It's mostly fabrication with a few chemical traces of truth.*"

" Let's match the tax cut and throw in a free lunch."

" And if it's voted down see where we can cash in on its failure."

" *Just try talking to your fellow diplomats that way and we'd be at war.*"

" It's our latest 'in flight noir'. It goes beautifully with our pumkin-colored accessories."

"What's this I hear about you being very happy here?"

" First off, you're probably asking yourself,
'What the hell am I doing here?' "

" *See if you can dumb it down a bit.* "

" *This is Freddie my ex-husband of many years.* "

" Mr. Stillman's an omnivorous reader. "

"*Freddy Farnsworth, oil, meet Eddie Wilson, bottled water,
I've been trying to get you fellows together for a long time.*"

" *It's another one of their so called damn friendly takeover offers.* "

" Here it is sir, an analysis of stock trends for the next thousand years."

" To my beautiful Lenna. I couldn't give you anything but love baby, cause that's the only thing I had plenty of, baby."

"...and if they should outlive me, I leave to my nephew, Freddie, my long-life electric bulbs."

" Here it is, ready for your signatures. Your premarital agreement
with a buyout if things go prematurely sour."

" Not guilty, guilty, such overused words."

" *Tell it to the court!* "

"And to my big mouth nephew,
I leave the remaining minutes on my cell phone."

" While you're at it, see if you can put a little magic back in our marriage."

"*Any apologies in order this morning, dear?*"

" Your name may have been Charlie,
but that was where the good times ended. "

" *We attribute our long marrige to staying power.*"

"Now what did I do?"

" *I'll say nothing to prejudice my case.* "

"*Married to the Internet*" cake

" *And now I pronounce you joint taxpayers.* "

"*I'm afraid there isn't much more we can do at these prices.*"

"Included is a video of the operation."

" *It was a great incentive. After two operations, the third one is free.* "

"*You don't deserve it, but I'm giving you a clean bill of health.*"

" *Let me skip my first opinion and give you my second.* "

" *I'm sorry the doctor's unavailable but his mother can see you.* "

" *That's Monique, she waltzed into my life and waltzed right out again.* "

"It's only fair to warn you.
I can't handle one on one relationships."

" *My wife has left me to my own devices.* "

" *Good heavens, Martha, we are entitled to a few honest differences.* "

" Marge, I want you to know, when it comes to women
I'm an investor not a trader."

"Elaine, I'm lost without you."

" My problem is I don't know where business ends and pleasure begins."

" *Sometimes I wonder if your criticism of me is as painful as you say.* "

"I don't know if it will work, you being visual and I verbal."

" It was love at first sight,
though I don't usually respond to visual stimulus."

"*My computer doesn't understand me.*"

" *I've never engaged in casual sex.*
Sex means too much to me."

" I'm what you'd call a monetary chemist.
I break everything down to dollars and cents."

" See, that's my bank down there.
I'm never more than five minutes away from my money."

"*I guess I'm just another one of those faceless bureaucrats.*"

" *Do remain standing.*
We're looking for someone who thinks well on his feet."

" We're looking for someone who thinks like you look
but doesn't happen to look like you think."

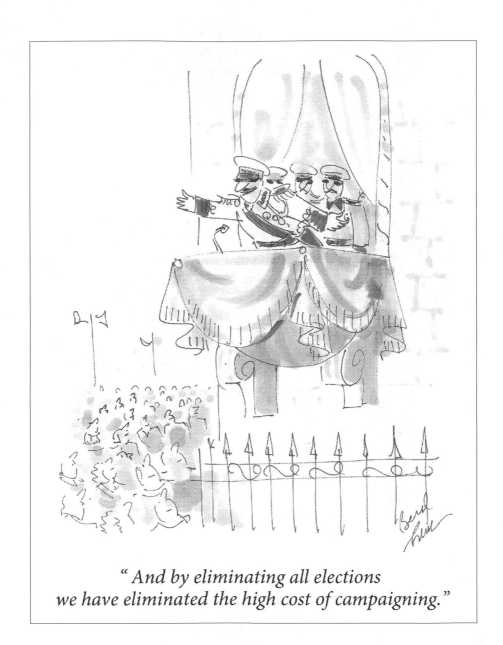

"*And by eliminating all elections
we have eliminated the high cost of campaigning.*"

" He jumped off the bandwagon."

"Just a 'yes' or 'no' to the following questions :
a. You can fool all the people some of the time ?
b. You can fool some of the people all the time ?
c. You can fool all the people all the time ? "

"*Tonight, 'Speak Out' brings you a wide spectrum of American opinion.*"

" *I'm sorry Albert it would never work.*
I'm upper management and you're middle."

" Wow! You're certainly one Republican who knows how to bridge the generation gap."

" *What say, you be my little Annie and I, your Daddy Warbucks?* "

" *Well, where the hell would you like to live happily ever after?* "

" *When I can't sleep, I count stars.*"

" I guess you can say I've always been goal oriented."

"Got it? Jab with your 'right' and follow through with your 'left'."

"*Ma'am, I'd stake my reputation on it.*"

"*Before they collect a dime,
see that there's a long drawn out court battle.*"

"*Figure any way I can leave it all to me?*"

" *I'm sure that any possible deficiency in this manuscript can be easily overcome by your public appearance.*"

"*It's so exciting meeting an author right at the very beginning of his fifteen minutes of fame.*"

" I call it 'Before The Sequel'."

"Ever ask yourself where we'd be without the comma?"

"*I dub you 'snowman'!*"

&Children

"*And never trust anyone under sixty.*"

" And remember, one and one doesn't always add up to two. "

" How I built my portfolio for a sound financial future."

" *Why don't we look at the report card as a temporary downturn in the second quarter?* "

" *This is Denise, my friend and financial advisor.* "

" *If I'm right, what do I win?* "

" *You promise but can you deliver ?* "

" *And stay young as long as possible.* "

" *Timmy is one of our latest internet service providers.*"

" And so the prince and the princess split with the princess receiving a divorce settlement worthy of her station and she lived happily ever after."

"*May I be excused? I'm still unwinding from the summer break.*"

" Can you make it an extra five
so as to maintain my competitive edge? "

"O.K. you be the policeman and you stop me for speeding
when I start crying you don't give me a ticket."

" *Mom just makes being a single parent look easy.* "

"I read at a second grade level and yes,
I am very satisfied with my education."

" *What's this about you wanting to buy yourself out of the family?* "

"Another twenty and I think I can buy the school election."

" *This time I'm letting the marriage play out before I evaluate it.* "

"*I know who did it but I can't tell you without divulging my sources.*"

"All right, but this is not going to play
well in my autobiography!"

" *Can I assume you're ready to settle your grievences out of court?* "

"Skip the nurturing. What do you think?"

"Come come, everyone has a dry period."

"So, you can play Mendelssohn's Violin Concerto
but I bet you can't tie your shoes?"

Photo of Bernard and Rhoda Schoenbaum on honeymoon 1948

Addendum

Bernard Schoenbaum

Bernard Schoenbaum was born and raised in New York City.
After receiving his art education at Parsons School of Design, he was a
free-lance advertising illustrator for many years.

Appearing in The New Yorker since 1974, he became a contract cartoonist
with more than 400 cartoons published. His cartoons have been reprinted in
books and periodicals worldwide and are also in many private collections.

His other endeavors included teaching the figure, life drawing, portrait
sketching, sculpture, oil painting and water colors. These have also been
privately collected.

He and his wife, Rhoda, a retired librarian, resided in Whitestone, New York
with a winter residence in West Palm Beach, Florida.

His three grown daughters are Laura Schoenbaum Rothenberg of Shirley,
New York, a graphic designer, Audrey Tufano of East Meadow, New York,
a computer technician, and Joyce Dara of Santa Monica, California,
an Instructional Director in Los Angeles Unified School District, California.
Granddaughter Cassandra Tufano is a graduate of SUNY Albany,

Bernard Schoenbaum
Memoir by Rhoda A.Schoenbaum

Artist, loving husband, father, grandfather.

His hands were clenched at the end leading me to think he was fighting,
yes, fighting the force that overpowered him.

During life he fought with trained pen, full heart and strong talent.
His sculpture, oil paintings, water colors and numerous portrait sketches
created for people throughout the world are a momentous legacy.

But the cartoons-over four hundred published in The New Yorker Magazine
(where he was a contracted cartoonist) as well as hundreds in other
periodicals and in countless books were his especial pride.

There is a Native American Proverb: " We will be known forever by the
tracks we leave." Bernard Schoenbaum left indelible, joyous art tracks.
Bernard was a true Artist and ethical human being with a sharp wit.
He was a husband, father and grandfather without peer.

A Letter written by
Alex Noel Watson
(Reproduced with author's permission)

ALEX NOEL WATSON   · June 2· 2010 ·   Noel Watson

Dear Rhoda,

Naturally, I was deeply sorry and grieved to receive the news of Bernie's passing. Many thanks for sending me the card with the information; very much appreciated. The next day I received from Henry Martin the obituary from The New York Times. My heartfelt sympathy to you all.

I always regarded Bernie as one of my very special New York friends and colleagues. New York was such a prominent and important period in my life, covering well over 25 years, and Bernie was a great shining star in it. I shall always treasure golden memories of him. And of my visits to your home.

I liked him enormously as a person and a friend; and I loved his work. To me he was one of the very top cartoonists in The New Yorker. His drawings always had a rare stylish elegance, and the sophistication of his art was matched by his brilliant, sophisticated ideas. And his cartoons always made me laugh. Nothing remotely as good is being published in the magazine today.

I am so glad that we kept in touch (a measure of our friendship), with you also, dear Rhoda, and I always looked forward to receiving from the Schoenbaums the lively and bracing cartoon card every New Year. Of course, I have kept all of those. Please continue to keep in touch, and I hope we shall meet again some day. And I shall never forget Bernie.

    With love from your friend,
      Alex

Obituary written by
Times Of London reporter

TIMES OF LONDON

Bernard Schoenbaum

October 6 2010 12:01AM

For almost 30 years Bernard Schoenbaum's work graced the pages of *The New Yorker*. What amused and sometimes discomfited his readers was a reflection of their own attitudes, ambitions, prejudices and conceits.

His subjects, or perhaps more accurately his targets, were drawn from the liberal East Coast and yet the traits he exposed — prosperous, knowing, ruthless, ironic, combative, crestfallen and cute — are universal ones. Schoenbaum and his contemporaries, Frank Modell, James Stevenson, Robert Weber and Lee Lorenz, were attuned to every nuance and quirk.

Born in Manhattan in 1920, Bernard was the elder son of Russian-Jewish émigrés. His younger brother Sam was a distinguished Shakespearean scholar. He was educated in the Bronx and at the Parsons School of Design, New York. Much of his career was as a freelance advertising illustrator but when his wife took a job as a librarian he was able to devote himself to cartooning. His other endeavours included teaching the figure, life drawing, portrait sketching, oil painting and watercolours. He also worked as a portraitist on cruise ships.

He contributed his first drawing (as *The New Yorker* preferred to call them) in 1974, when the celebrated William Shawn was still editor, and Lee Lorenz the arts editor. He was to contribute 463 cartoons to the magazine. He also contributed to *Barron's* and *The Wall Street Journal*.

Some of his earliest drawings and a sprinkling of all his work were captionless. His approach was literal while his style was a soft, fluid line and wash. He captured a northeastern knowingness; a world of men in tweed sports jackets, soft plaid hats and bad haircuts such that the reader would be taken in immediately and ready to laugh even before coming to the caption.

His cartoons embraced the world of parties and romance, commerce and employment, parents and children. The children were so worldly: a young boy says to his father who is reading his son's school report, "It's just a correction. The fundamentals are still good"; a little girl in bed talking to her father who has read her a fairytale, "It sounds a little too perfect. What's the downside?"; while another little girl says to her mother as they confront each other over a broken biscuit jar in the kitchen "Circumstantial. You haven't proved linkage."

Schoenbaum was as sharp in the office — an executive to others meeting around a table: "To pacify our shareholders, it's been suggested that one of us goes to jail." One businessman to another in a plush office says: "I'll level with you, Charlie. I'm going to let money get in the way of our friendship." A suited man at his desk on the phone says: "Joyce, I'm so madly in love with you I can't eat, I can't sleep, I can't live without you. But that's not why I called."

And the enduring issue of matrimony — a woman to a man at a smart restaurant: "Is this a real proposal, or are you off your medication?"; and a man to a woman as he proposes to her in a restaurant: "Say yes. I need a win."

His last cartoon, published in 2002, rather fittingly depicted two angels in Heaven; one saying to the other: "At least there's one place that's not youth-oriented."

As *The New Yorker's* current cartoon editor, Bob Mankoff, observed: "He was a sweet and gentle man. His humour did not look down on people, just a bit sideways."

Schoenbaum is survived by his wife, Rhoda (whom he married in 1948) and their three daughters.

Bernard Schoenbaum, cartoonist, was born on August 8, 1920. He died on May 7, 2010, aged 89

Bernard Schoenbaum's
Cartoons in Books

Titles	Pages
All You Can Eat: A Feast of Great Food Cartoons	unpaged - one
Art and Artists: New Yorker Cartoons from The Melvin R. Seiden Coll.	78, 00
Barrons Book of Cartoons	26, 30, 33, 40, 53, 75, 77, 85, 96
Books Books Books: A Hilarious Collection of Literary Cartoons	unpaged- three
Cats Cats Cats: A Collection of Great Cat Cartoons	16, 26, 55, 67, 83, 97,136, 159, 193, 200, 201, 211, 234
Dogs Dogs Dogs: A Collection of Great Dog Cartoons	unpaged - twenty cartoons
Fathers and Sons: It's a Funny Relationship	unpaged - two
Golf Golf Golf	66, 92, 96
Ho Ho Ho: A Stocking-Full of Christmas Cartoons	unpaged - two
Lawyers Lawyers Lawyers: a Cartoon Collection	67, 00
Moms Moms Moms: A Mirthful Merriment of Cartoons	unpaged - two
Movies Movies Movies: A Hilarious Collection of Cartoons	10, 14, 32, 60, 103
Now That You Can Walk, Go Get Me A Beer: A Book for Dads	unpaged - two
Play Ball: An All Star Lineup of Baseball Cartoons	unpaged - three
The American Cartoon Album	unpaged - four
The Art in Cartooning	160, 207
The Complete Cartoons of The New Yorker	400, 458, 501, 516, 539, 566, 583 plus 450 on disc
The New Yorker 75th Anniversary Cartoon Collection	28, 146, 181, 186, 221, 229, 247, 249, 279
The Big New Yorker Book of Cats	72
The New Yorker Book of Baseball Cartoons	1
The New Yorker Book of Business Cartoons	94, 110
The New Yorker Book of Cat Cartoons	38, 68, 84
The New Yorker Book of Dog Cartoons	11, 44
The New Yorker Book of Kid Cartoons	30, 84, 125
The New Yorker Book of Literary Cartoons	75, 89, 101
The New Yorker Book of Money Cartoons	13, 77, 89, 98
The New Yorker Book of Political Cartoons	3, 29, 96, 110
The New Yorker Book of Teacher Cartoons	42, 55, 57
The New Yorker Book of Technology Cartoons	8, 80
The New Yorker Book of True Love Cartoons	36, 100
The New Yorker Cartoon Album 1975-1985	unpaged - four
The Wall Street Journal Carton Portfolio	unpaged - one
The Wall Street Journal Portfolio of Woman in Business	59, 00
They'll Outgrow It and Other Myths: the Best Cartoons for Parents	82, 00
Why Are Your Papers in Order? Cartoons for 1984	unpaged - four

Printed in the United States
By Bookmasters